Samuel G. Buckingham

A Memorial of the Pilgrim Fathers

Samuel G. Buckingham

A Memorial of the Pilgrim Fathers

ISBN/EAN: 9783337288020

Printed in Europe, USA, Canada, Australia, Japan

Cover: Foto ©Andreas Hilbeck / pixelio.de

More available books at **www.hansebooks.com**

A

MEMORIAL

OF THE

Pilgrim Fathers.

A

MEMORIAL

OF THE

Pilgrim Fathers.

BY

S. G. BUCKINGHAM,

PASTOR OF THE SOUTH CHURCH,
SPRINGFIELD, MASS.

———————◆———————

SPRINGFIELD:
SAMUEL BOWLES & COMPANY, PRINTERS.
1867.

Preface.

THE Congregational Council which met at Boston in the summer of 1865, recommended that $200,000 be raised to aid feeble churches in erecting houses of worship, and that a collection be taken up by all the churches of our denomination in behalf of this object, on the 17th of December, the Sabbath preceding Forefather's Day. This sketch of those men, their character, principles and achievements, was prepared for that occasion, and with some additions and omissions, is now printed particularly for distribution among the pastor's own people.

In order to give it more value and furnish further information upon these subjects to those who desire it, reference is made to a few easily accessible books. Young's Chronicles of the Pilgrim Fathers, containing Gov. Bradford's History of the Plymouth Colony, and Edward Winslow's Brief Narration, (both of whom came over in the Mayflower), furnishes, in connection with the full and accurate notes of the Editor, abundant and reliable information in regard to the emigration of the Pilgrims; while Neale's History of the Puritans, is generally regarded as the fullest and best authority respecting the state of things in England, which led to this emigration. When these books are referred to, the particular reference is given.

If this tribute to our Fathers, should do anything to interest others more deeply in their history, or promote a better understanding of their principles and motives, or cause their institutions to be held in higher estimation, or especially lead to any imitation of their piety and self-sacrificing spirit, the wishes of the author would be fully realized.

Discourse.

THE story of our *Pilgrim Fathers*, and their settlement upon these shores, is as familiar to us as an oft-repeated tale. Still it is a tale of such Christian heroism, and grand achievement, that it will never lose its interest with mankind, and least of all to us their children. We owe so much to them, and to the God who raised them up, and inspired them with such sentiments, and guided them to this land, and guarded them through all their perils, and enabled them to plant here a pure church, and a Christian Commonwealth, that we shall never tire of recounting their deeds and God's mercies. Nor should we fail to instruct our children in this history, or to teach it to the world.

Driven out from England because they could not conscientiously conform to the requirements of the Established Church, the Puritans went over to Holland and established themselves for a few years at Leyden. But finding it difficult, as they tell us, to support themselves in that country, and that few were willing to join them there, and that as they grew old, their company was in danger of becoming extinct, or at least of being scattered, and that their children were corrupted by the bad influences around them, and desiring also to live under the protection of England, and to retain the language and name of Englishmen, and on account of their inability to give their children such an education as they had

1*

themselves received, and owing to their grief at the profana-
tion of the Sabbath around them, and having lastly, (as they
express it) "a great hope and inward zeal of laying some
good foundation, or at least to make some way thereunto, for
the propagating and advancing the gospel of the kingdom of
Christ in these remote parts of the earth, though they should
be but as stepping-stones unto others for performing of so
great a work;"—(Young's Chron., p. 45-47,) they determined to remove to some other country. At first they
thought seriously of Guyana, in South America, a glowing
account of which had just been published by Sir Walter
Raleigh : but the objections to it were, that such hot climates
were not likely to agree with their northern constitutions, and
that the jealous Spaniards would never suffer them to live
there in peace, especially if they prospered. Next they turn-
ed their attention to Virginia, where the attempt was already
making to plant an English Colony ; but they feared that if
they "lived among the English which were there planted, or
so near them as to be under their government, they should be
in as great danger to be troubled and persecuted for their
cause of religion, as if they lived in England, and it might be
worse, and if they lived too far off, they should neither have
succor nor defence from them."—(Young's Chron., p. 54).
It was finally decided to settle farther north, and beyond the
reach of the Virginia Colony, and in a part of the country
which they called New England. They little knew what a
rugged country it was, and what a rigid climate they must
endure, and how many savage tribes they would encounter,
but they valued nothing so much as civil and religious freedom, and they feared savages, and cold, and a sterile soil, less
than the enemies of their faith and freedom.

So after much negotiation with the government of England,
and with the Land Company under whose protection they
were to emigrate, and whose charter was to secure to them

certain rights, William Brewster, the Ruling Elder of the Leyden Church, and somewhat less than one-half of its members, embarked for their new home, while John Robinson, the pastor, and the rest of the Church, remained behind until they could make their arrangements to follow. That *embarkation* at Delft-Haven, after they had observed a day of fasting and prayer, and their pastor had preached to them that sermon, so full of encouragement and good counsel, and they had poured out their supplications to God in behalf of one another with many tears, and they left so regretfully "that goodly and pleasant city which had been their resting-place near twelve years," and where they say, "they knew they were *pilgrims*, and looked not much on those things, but lifted up their eyes to heaven, their dearest country, and quieted their spirits:"—(Young's Chron., p. 87,)—that last scene upon the shore, when all their friends were gathered about them to take leave of them, and, as one of their own number tells us, after a "night spent with little sleep by the most, but with friendly entertainment, and Christian discourse, and other real expressions of true Christain love, the next day the wind being fair, they went on board, and their friends with them, when truly doleful was the sight of that sad and mournful parting; to hear what sighs, and sobs, and prayers did sound among them; what tears did gush from every eye, and pithy speeches pierced each other's heart; that sundry of the Dutch strangers, that stood on the quay as spectators, could not refrain from tears; yet comfortable and sweet it was to see such lively and true expressions of true and unfeigned love:— but the tide, which stays for no man, calling them away, that were thus loth to depart, their reverend pastor, falling down on his knees, and they all with him, with watery cheeks, commended them, with most fervent prayers, to the Lord and his blessing; and then with mutual embraces and many tears, they took leave of one another, which proved to be their last leave to many of them:"—(Young's Chron., p. 88,)—this event, so touching in interest, and so sublime in its object and motives, and so important in our history, and likely to be of such influence upon the welfare of our race, has become the theme of painting and poetry, and may well thrill our hearts with admiration and gratitude, as we recognize in these men our sires, and discern in the Providence that was guiding them hither blessings for ourselves, unspeakable blessings, and benefits scarcely inferior to mankind at large.

They had great difficulty in setting out on their *voyage*, being twice compelled to put back on account of the unseaworthiness of one of their vessels, and after dismissing this ship, and crowding as many of its passengers as possible on board of the other ships, they finally set sail for their strange home. They had already been detained a full month, and instead of arriving here, as they should have done, in the last of September, or during the charming weather of October, it was bleak November before they approached the coast, and sharp winter was upon them before they had found and fixed upon a place of settlement. They had had a long and stormy passage of sixty-four days, when to their joy they fell in with Cape Cod and found shelter in its hospitable bay. Here first of all they "fell down upon their knees and blessed the Lord, the God of Heaven, who had brought them over the vast and furious ocean, and delivered them from all perils and miseries thereof, again to set their feet on the firm and stable earth, their proper element."

One of our stern winters was upon them. The whole country was full of woods and thickets, giving to everything a wild and savage hue. Within those thickets lurked more savage men, so that they could not land except as armed, and in companies. The Captain of the ship was anxious to get rid of them, and it was already rumored that if they did not soon provide a place for settlement, he would set them out upon the shore and leave them. Behind them was the ocean, from whose perils they had just escaped, and which was now a gulf to separate them from all the rest of the world. True, they had good friends in the brethren they left behind; but they had little power to help them, or even themselves. And the Land Company that sent them out were not likely to do much for them, when they sujected them to such hard conditions, and were more bent upon making money, than founding a Puritan Colony. Their prospects were dark indeed; "and what," as they say, "could now sustain them, but the spirit of God and his grace."

With firm faith in that God, and with the full conviction that they were under his guidance in this undertaking, and with a sincere desire to extend their Redeemer's Kingdom among men, they bravely confronted the difficulties before them, and set about accomplishing their mission.

There lies the Mayflower; a name so sacred to our hearts as the ark in which our faith, and ecclesiastical government, and substantially the gem of our civil institutions, were preserved; a vessel of only 180 tons; less than the average size of the fishing-smacks that now sail in such numbers from that harbor to the Grand Bank; but with her one hundred emigrants on board, containing within her poor accommodations, we must think, more of sincere faith, and religious motive, and Christian enterprise, and more of truth, and freedom, and benevolence, than were ever gathered in one ship before since the Savior sailed the sea of Galilee. They are imperfect men, and have been trained in a rough school, but they have as much of charity and gentleness as most, and more of conscientiousness, and courage, and faith, and hope, than any. They owe supreme allegiance to Christ, and identify themselves with his kingdom, and to be loyal to this king, and promote his cause in the earth, is alike their purpose, and their inspiration. They are such men as *Carver*, and *Bradford*, and

Winslow, and *Brewster*, and such women as their wives, some of them of gentle blood and tender nurture, but all full of fortitude, and firm in their Puritan faith, and wholly consecrated to this Christian enterprise, even though they should fall, as so many of them will before the coming spring, like flowers smitten by the cold of winter. It is a noble company. They have firm faith in God; implicit and absolute faith. They believe in truth, and especially in God's revealed truth. They will uphold the rights of men; man's civil rights, and religious freedom. And they would, if possible, leave to their children, and to the world, a purer church, and a better modeled state, even though they should perish in the undertaking. And so consecrated are they to this enterprise, that neither the gloomy wilderness, nor the prowling savages, nor the appalling winter, nor the awful sense of loneliness and homesickness which these poor exiles will experience when they come to find themselves alone upon the shore, can deter them from it, and when the ship returns, not one of their number will return in her.

They land upon the beach to find wood and water, and refresh themselves. They draw up their shallop, or large boat, upon the shore to repair it, for it is in this that they must explore the coast and fix upon a place of settlement. They make short excursions into the country, and discover the Indians, who are to prove such cunning and merciless foes, and find some Indian corn, which they greatly need, and for which they are careful to pay the owners months after, and admire the strange trees and vines, and the abundance of fowl and deer, and the springs of fresh water. Then when their boat is finished it is resolved to send forth a company upon a longer excursion of discovery—the expedition which made its way to Plymouth harbor, and finally fixed upon that as their home. Two hundred and forty-five years ago to-day, Wednesday, December 6th, in Old Style, if you could have looked upon the scene, over that broad expanse of waters, now relieved by so many snow-white sails, and the smoke cloud of so many steamers, you would have seen that solitary pilgrim ship at anchor just within the point, and this sail boat, with a company of eighteen on board, trying to beat out of the harbor. It is with difficulty that they clear this sandy point, and when they do, and get under the weather shore, and find smoother water and better sailing, still it is very cold, and "the water freezes on their clothes and makes them like coats of iron," as they coast along the shore, and stop occasionally to explore a bay, or to land and find out whether the place is a suitable one for a settlement. On Friday afternoon a storm overtakes them, and comes near wrecking them, but a merciful Providence drives them into Plymouth harbor, and in the growing darkness of the evening and the rain they come to anchor, and effect a landing upon Clark's Island. Here they spend Saturday, and keep the Sabbath "according to the commandment," and on Monday, finding the harbor a good one, and the location inviting, they fix upon this as their future home, come on shore, and their feet for the first time step upon Plymouth Rock.

And now, who were these exiles, that they were unable to live in England? Were they not Englishmen, and entitled to all the rights and privileges of Englishmen? Certainly. Were they people of bad morals and scandalous lives? By no means. The magistrates of Leyden said of them: "These English have lived among us now this twelve years, and yet we never had any suit or accusation come against any of them." (Young's Chron., p. 39.) In a sermon afterwards preached in London before the Lord Mayor and Aldermen, and both Houses of Parliament and the Westminster Assembly of Divines, constituting the most remarkable auditory which the world could then have brought together, the preacher said: "I have lived in a country where in seven years I never saw a beggar, nor heard an oath, nor looked upon a drunkard. That country was New England." Were they mad reformers, and the enemies of good government? No. These, and the emigration that followed, all belonged to that party in England of whom Hume says, though he had no sympathy with their religious faith: "The precious spark of liberty had been kindled by the Puritans alone," and admits that to them "the English owe the whole freedom of their Constitution." Were they deserving of censure for their mode of living? Not as compared with their opponents. "It was a distinguishing mark of a Puritan, in those times," we are told, "to see him going to church twice a day, with his Bible under his arm, while others were at plays and interludes, at revels and walking in the fields, or at diversions of bowling, fencing, &c., on the evening of the Sabbath. These with their families, were employed in reading the Scriptures, singing Psalms, catechising their children, repeating sermons and prayer." (Neale. vol. I., p. 399.) Were they base and ignorant people? Certainly not, for they especially advocated learning and an educated ministry, and when "the body of the conforming clergy were so ignorant and illiterate that many who had the cure of souls were incapable of preaching, or even of reading to the edification of their hearers," "the non-conformist ministers, under the character of curates, or lecturers, supplied the defects of these idle drones, and by their warm and affectionate preaching, gained the hearts of the people." (Neale, vol. I., p. 230.) Were they a rude and vulgar class of people? In scholarship they produced Milton, and Sir Walter Raleigh, and Lightfoot, and Locke; and such statesmen as Hampden, and Pym, and Sir Harry Vane, and Cromwell; and such magistrates as Carver, and Bradford, and Winthrop, and Eaton; and such ministers as John Robinson, and Brewster, and John Cotton, and Hooker, and Davenport. Were they a poor and thriftless class of the population of England? By no means, for "it was computed," says Neale, "that the four settlements of New England, viz. : Plymouth, Massachusetts, Connecticut, and New Haven, all of which were accomplished before the civil wars, (or within twenty years after the settlement of Plymouth,) drained England of £400,000 or £500,000 sterling, a very great sum for those days ; and if the persecutions of the Puritans had continued twelve years longer, it is thought that a fourth part of the riches of the kingdom would have passed out of it through this channel." Were they the slaves of superstition, and miserable fanatics in religion? Far from it. They held to certain superstitious notions, like that of witchcraft, as all in that age did, but judged by the age in which they lived :— which is the only fair mode of estimating them aright:—they had the least superstition about them of any class in those days. They certainly did not believe in the divine right of kings, or in the divine right of bishops, as so many did ; nor did they believe it necessary for ministers to wear certain vestments in order to make their services of any worth ; nor did they use the sign of the cross to drive out devils and expel diseases, and keep off witches ; nor would they kneel at the sacrament, as if the bread had become a god, like so many others. They were confessedly the sturdiest theologians of their age, if not of any age, and were bravely endeavoring to harmonize reason with revelation, and systematize, and explain, and justify all the great doctrines of the Bible, in connection with the principles of human philosophy, and had so far succeeded, that their system of Calvinism must be admitted to be the most intellectual, and well digested, and complete theology, that the church has known. Were they the enemies of their country, that she should deal with them so rigidly, and finally banish them? O, no! In spite of this unnatural cruelty of a mother, casting out her own

2

children, they cherished toward her a filial reverence and affection, which is truly touching. They felt as Higginson did when leaving England and her shores were fading from his view; calling his children and the other passengers around him, he exclaimed: "We will not say as the separatists are wont to say, at their leaving England: 'Farewell, Babylon! Farewell, Rome!' But we will say: 'Farewell, dear England! Farewell, the Church of God in England, and all the Christian friends there.' We do not go to New England as separatists from the Church of England; but we go to practice the positive part of Church Reformation, and to propagate the gospel in America."—(Hall's Puritans and their Principles.) What then was the crime for which such men were driven into exile, and for which they were punished so severely before they left? It was for non-conformity to the established religion of the state.

The Church of England was a hierarchy, as its civil government was a monarchy. It was a complicated system of ecclesiastical government, made up of bishops and all the various orders of such an establishment, at the head of which was the reigning monarch, whatever might be his character, and its authority was enforced by all the pains and penalties of the civil power. It was a state establishment which the state organized, and controlled, and corrupted necessarily by this very control. The Church of England, at this time, was only imperfectly reformed, and still retained many of the errors and superstitious practices of the Church of Rome. Indeed some of these practices had been retained by Elizabeth on purpose to please her Roman Catholic subjects, and with the hope of uniting all in the same ecclesiastical establishment. Arch Bishop Land, especially, was bent upon bringing back some of the most objectionable of these practices; such as the substitution of an altar for the communion table; the wearing of all the Catholic vestments; the use of pictures and images; the sign of the cross; and kneeling before the bread in the sacrament. And these observances were to be enforced, whatever scruples one might have in regard to them.

The Pilgrims, on the other hand, were *Congregationalists.* They held that every church had the right to govern itself, according to the practice of the New Testament churches; that there was no Scriptural authority for bishops; that such ceremonies were superstitious, and as they had been used for superstitious purposes, and could not continue to be used without injury, they were sinful. And as they could not admit the truth of such prelatical claims and practice such superstitious rites, they could not conscientiously conform to the requirements of the State Church.*

But they were required to conform, and that under the severest penalties. And the story of what they suffered, and

---

* As showing the scruples and spirit of these men, let me refer to the examination of one of them in the Bishop's Court, as given by Neale, (Vol. 1, p. 173), who had been cited three times the same year to appear there, for refusing the apparel, the cross in baptism and kneeling at the sacrament, which were required of him. The Bishop was disposed to deal mildly with him, and after arguing the matter at length, he said: " Well, you must yield somewhat to me, and I will yield somewhat to you. I will not trouble you for the cross in baptism, but if you will *wear the surplice but sometimes,* it shall suffice." To which the Puritan minister replies: " I can't consent to wear it, it is against my conscience; I trust by the help of God, I shall never put on that sleeve, which is a mark of the beast." " Will you leave your flock for the surplice?" says the Bishop. " Nay," answers the non-conformist. " Will you persecute me from my flock for a surplice? I love my flock in Jesus Christ, and had rather have my right arm cut off than be removed from them." He was let off at that time, but a few months later he was summoned before the same Court and silenced, and deprived of his living, and driven to seek his bread in another country, though the Bishop owned he was a divine of good learning, a ready memory, and well qualified for the pulpit.

of the number who suffered, fills a large and melancholy page of history. They were forbidden to hold little religious meetings. They were fined and imprisoned for not attending upon the services of the Established Church. Their ministers were forbidden to preach and ejected from their livings. And for venturing to preach afterwards they were thrown into prison, and banished from the country. One of the acts of Parliament, passed during Queen Elizabeth's reign—the most intolerant and cruel that ever disgraced the statute book of a Protestant and free people—was: "That if any person above the age of sixteen shall obstinately refuse to repair to some church, chapel, or usual place of common prayer to hear divine service, for the space of one month, without lawful cause; or shall at any time, forty days after the end of this session, by·printing, writing, or express words, go about to persuade any of her Majesty's subjects to deny, withstand, or impugn her Majesty's power or authority in causes ecclesiastical; or shall dissuade them from coming to church to hear divine service, or receive the communion as the law directs; or shall be present at any unlawful assembly, conventicle, or meeting, under color or pretence of any exercise of religion; that every person so offending, and lawfully convicted, shall be committed to prison *without bail*, till they shall conform and yield themselves to come to church, and make the following declaration of their conformity:

'I, A. B., do humbly confess and acknowledge, that I have grievously offended God in contemning her Majesty's godly and lawful government and authority, by absenting myself from church, and from hearing divine service, contrary to the godly laws and statutes of the realm, and in frequenting disorderly and unlawful conventicles, under pretence and color of exercise of religion; and I am heartily sorry for the same, and do acknowledge and testify in my conscience, that no other person has, or ought to have, authority over Her

Majesty. And I do promise and protest, without any dissimulation or color of dispensation, that from henceforth I will obey Her Majesty's statutes and laws in repairing to church and hearing divine service; and to my utmost endeavor will maintain and defend the same."

"But in case the offender against this statute, being lawfully convicted, shall not submit and sign the Declaration within three months, THEN THEY SHALL ABJURE THE REALM, AND GO INTO PERPETUAL BANISHMENT. And if they do not depart within the time limited by the quarter sessions, or justices of peace; or, if they return at any time afterwards without the Queen's license, *they shall suffer death without benefit of clergy.*" (Neale, vol. 1, p. 362.) Nor was this unmeaning threatening. Numbers were banished, and by a refinement of cruelty, were refused the privilege of going to America, where their friends already were. Numbers more lay in prison for years, and often without power to obtain either bail or trial. Some, like Greenwood and Penry, were put to death. Two thousand of the ablest and best ministers of the Established Church were driven out from the ministry, and silenced, during this period, because they could not with truth subscribe to such declarations, nor conscientiously conform to the requirements of such a church. As King James said, to some of them who conferred with him about this matter, "If this be all your party have to say, I will make them conform, or I will harry them [worry, torment them,] out of the land; or else hang them; that is all." And this was what led some of these ministers, with their people, to flee to the continent, and finally made so many of them banish themselves to this wilderness. They preferred civil and religious freedom, even though it were in a wilderness, and among savages, to such intolerance and oppression in their native land, and at the hands of their own countrymen. They believed in a sim-

2*

pler and more scriptural form of church government, and purer and less superstitious worship ; and they had an idea that an intelligent and Christian community might be trusted to elect their own rulers, and make their own laws — in short, they believed in " a church without a bishop, and a state without a king ;" and they came here to undertake, with God's blessing, to organize both. And how well they succeeded, let the results of their undertaking show.

The *Results* of this Pilgrim Emigration and Settlement demand special consideration. For results, after all, furnish us with the most satisfactory means of judging of men, and of their institutions. Self-willed and impracticable men, when they come to build up, instead of opposing and pulling down, show their defects of character. Theories, that look well upon paper, are found ill-adapted to human wants, or to human nature. Institutions that seem desirable are proved useless, or experience shows that they can never be permanently established. But when an experiment has been thoroughly made, and time enough has elapsed to show what results naturally and necessarily follow, then we place confidence in our judgments concerning causes and influences and agencies. To be sure, other agencies may counteract or modify those on trial; still we can generally detect the influence of each, and judge pretty correctly of their tendency and power ; just as the clear waters of the Mississippi can be traced long after they mingle with the turbid Missouri, and there is no mistaking the drift of this combined current towards the gulf, though obstructions and eddies may set it back in places. So, through all our history, it is easy enough to trace the influence of the Pilgrims, and their ideas and characteristics and work, and to see where their influence has been the strongest, what kind of churches it builds up, and what legislation it secures, and what state of society it produces. And now it seems no longer difficult, in view of such results, to form a just estimate of these men, and of their work in settling this country. Need one doubt any longer whether the Puritans were essentially right in their protest against the absolute power of kings, and the spiritual despotism of a hierarchy? Need one doubt any longer whether men are capable of governing themselves in both Church and State, or suppose that freedom necessarily leads to heresy and impiety in the one, any more than to license and revolution in the other? Or need one doubt any longer what sort of a population, and what state of society, such civil and religious institutions will produce, and whether, on the whole, any other form of government, or religious faith, have shown themselves to be preferable to these?

Foreigners are accustomed to regard our experiment as not yet complete, and to think that time enough has not yet elapsed to enable us to judge well of results. True we cannot boast, like Russia, or England, of a thousand years of national existence, nor point, with the Jews, to institutions that remained essentially unchanged for fifteen hundred years. But if we reckon existence, not so much by years, as by intellectual activity and experience, and events, and achievements, it may be a question whether our national life of two hundred and fifty years will not compare with some of the longest of them. In the dull and changeless East, and in patriarchal times, when nothing ever happened more important than the death of a camel, or the birth of a child; for people seldom died in those days; was a century in reality any longer than some of these decades of years? And why may we not speak of results as well as they? Of course we are liable to changes, and even to revolutions, like other nations. But if "nothing is ever settled until it is settled right," we have quite as many of the elements of permanence as any government, we think. We may become a monarchy again, and adopt a hierarchy, but neither looks very likely at present. It seems quite as likely that some of the old kingdoms of the world will become republics, and some of the ecclesiastical establishments of history become simple and self-governed churches. At any rate, we know no reason why the results already obtained, and the experiment so far as made, should not claim respect, and be used to illustrate the character, and principles, and institutions, of our Pilgrim Fathers.

What then have been the Results of this emigration of the Pilgrims?

1. *They have settled this country.*

This was not the first, or the only settlement made here. But most of them were failures, and such as were permanent never had any such influence in securing this result, or ever left so much of its impress upon the nation, as this colony.

More than a century before the pilgrims came, the Spaniards had taken possession of Florida, and attempted to found a colony there, but they were driven off and their leader mortally wounded by the natives. Eighty years before, the Spaniard, De Soto, with several hundred followers, had fought his way to the Mississippi and penetrated two hundred miles beyond, but only to return to the river and die there, and his discouraged followers to abandon the expedition. The French Huguenots, who first settled at Port Royal, in South Carolina, and afterwards in Florida, in 1565, were massacred by the Spaniards; while of Sir Walter Raleigh's settlement on Roanoke Island, in North Carolina, in 1585, in a few years not a trace remained. The English settlement at the mouth of the Kennebec in Maine, and the French settlement at Mount Desert, both of which preceded the one at Plymouth, were soon abandoned, or broken up. The Virginia colony at

Jamestown, may be said to have been established, and was thirteen years older than the Plymouth colony; and the Dutch had discovered the Hudson, and begun to erect their trading posts, and make arrangements for colonization, even before the pilgrims came. But after all, it may well be doubted, whether either of them would have been permanently successful, had it not been for the success of this new colony, and of the other colonies, which it soon gathered about it. The successful settlement at Plymouth, led in eight years to the planting of the Massachusetts colony, and within ten years more, to the planting successively of the colonies of Connecticut, Rhode Island and New Haven. So that within twenty years after the landing of the pilgrims, twenty-one thousand persons, almost exclusively English, and mostly of the Puritan faith, had come over and found a home in this new country. After that came on the troubles and civil wars in England, and such emigration almost entirely ceased, and was never resumed until about forty years ago. But that first emigration was sufficient to demonstrate the practicability of the enterprise, and to ensure the settlement of the whole country, and to determine the character of its population, and the nature of its institutions.

At that time the subject of colonization was less understood, and attended with more difficulties, than at present. The ocean was more formidable, and a voyage across it more uncomfortable and dangerous, than it is now. The popular dread of the sea, such small and frail ships, and a passage of nine or ten weeks, instead of about as many days, were great hindrances to the founding and successful establishment of a distant colony. Besides, governments did less then, than they do now, to foster such enterprises. They were quite apt to hamper them with restrictions upon their legislation and trade, and when they began to prosper, and especially to show any independence, instead of tolerating it, and regarding it as a part of their own prosperity, they too often became jealous of them, and reduced their privileges, and took away their charters, as these colonies found by sad experience.

This whole land was at that time a wilderness. It was un-inhabited except by the savages who roamed over it, and the wild beasts which they hunted for a support. Its lands were all uncultivated, except as the natives raised a little Indian corn to eke out the uncertain supplies of the chase. Its for-ests were unused, and so extensive and dense as seriously to interfere with settlement. Its sea-coasts and bays, so favor-ably situated for commerce, had no trade whatever, and the wide waste of waters was not relieved by a solitary sail, or steamer, while the rivers and inland waters that now float such cargoes of grain, and iron, and coal, and so many manu-factured articles, and foreign products, and such crowds of passengers, had never been rippled by any keel save that of the Indian's canoe. Its mineral resources were all undevel-oped and unknown. Its water power was all unused and un-thought of. Its prairies, capable of feeding half the world, were uncultivated, and its cotton-fields, whose product has since claimed to control the markets of the world, were all untilled. It was wholly a wilderness, unsettled and unsub-dued. The country had not even been explored, and the place where these emigrants settled, was apparently fixed upon quite as much by chance; or rather, by God's good providence over them; and by the necessity of making for themselves a home somewhere immediately, as by any peculiar advantages which it offered. The coast was rough and forbid-ding. The climate was rigid, and seemed likely to require all that could be raised during one-half of the year, to keep its in-habitants from perishing during the other half. The process of acclimation was also to be gone through with; a process so little understood then, but so trying to foreigners under the most favorable circumstances; and which, with their privations and hardships, would lay so many of their number in their graves, before spring came.

And then they were surrounded by those Indians, so numerous, so jealous, so treacherous, so revengeful, so cruel; how could they ever expect, for themselves and their families, to escape massacre, and that their settlement would not be broken up? They were obliged to till their fields with their fire-arms within reach, and when they came to church they left their guns in the porch, with a sentinel to watch against the approach of their foe. And yet with all their precautions, how often were their towns invaded and burnt—as this town was—and sometimes their inhabitants carried away captives, like those of Deerfield, and how much oftener was the solitary settler waylaid and massacred, and his family tomahawked and scalped by his side?

In spite of such perils and hardships, these settlers prosecuted their undertaking, and never seem to have faltered in it for one moment. When the Mayflower returned to England the next spring, not an individual of the colony returned in her. Although it was after that terrible winter, when, as one of them describes it, they "died sometimes two or three a day, and of a hundred persons scarce fifty remained, and the living were scarce able to bury the dead, and the well not sufficient to tend the sick," and when they felt obliged to level their graves, lest the Indians should find out how their number was reduced, there was no disposition whatever to abandon the enterprise. They felt themselves called of God, as much as His people of old, to lay the foundations of a new church, and a Christian Commonwealth, and they vigorously prosecuted their work until they saw those foundations well laid, and the walls rising rapidly above them. They made their settlement a permanent one. They demonstrated the success of the experiment. They led the way for so many other colonists, and for so many others of like principles with themselves, and thus did so much to determine the character and the institutions of this nation. And one of the results has been, the virtual settlement, and such a settlement, of this whole country.

From that time our population has been steadily, and of late rapidly, spreading itself over the whole land. New England has already a pretty dense population, and there is a broad belt, including the Northern and Middle States, and stretching from the coast to the Mississippi, which abounds with inhabitants, and comfort, and thrift, and all the elements and institutions of a Christian civilization. From the Atlantic coast the tide of emigration has set round upon the shores of the Pacific, where cities are already built, and new States founded, and the waves from both the Atlantic and the Pacific are flowing inland, until there will soon be no habitable spot witin this vast area, that has not been reached, and fertilized by such civilizing and Christianizing influences. "The wilderness and the solitary place shall be glad for them, and the desert shall rejoice and blossom as the rose. It shall blossom abundantly, and rejoice even with joy and singing; the glory of Lebanon shall be given unto it, the excellency of Carmel and Sharon; they shall see the glory of the Lord, and the excellency of our God."

And it is remarkable how this original population, and its influence, have diffused themselves throughout the entire nation. The original emigration to New England was almost entirely English and Protestant, and even Puritan in its character. After the battles of Dunbar and Worcester, Cromwell sent some four or five hundred of his Scotch prisoners to Boston. After the revocation of the edict of Nantes, about a hundred and fifty families of French Huguenots came to Massachusetts; and a hundred and twenty Scotch-Irish families settled in New Hampshire. With these exceptions, all the foreign elements that are now found here, have come in within the last forty years.—(Palfrey's History of New England, Preface.) So distinctly Puritan was our original population. And now it is estimated that of all the present inhabitants of this country, one-third of them are of New England origin. Of the thirty million who now compose this nation, it is not too much to say, that ten million of them have Puritan blood in their veins. And if there is any truth in such popular sayings as these: "Blood tells;" "Blood is thicker than water;" may we not hope that some of the Puritan traits and characteristics will always be transmitted to this nation, and make us somewhat like our ancestry, and as there is more of sympathy and affection among kindred, that our sameness of stock, and common origin, will help to bind us together, and cement our unity as a people.

It is certainly noticeable and cause for thankfulness, that when the Spaniards had discovered this continent, and planted their colonies in South America and Mexico so long before our fathers came here, and when the French subsequently obtained possession of the Canadas, and established their military posts along the Lakes and the Mississippi, from Montreal to New Orleans, neither of them ever obtained possession of the country to settle it under Roman Catholic influences. God seems to have studiously shut them out from its ample territory and boundless resources, that he might give it to a people of his own, whom he then had in training, and whom he would one day introduce here, bringing with them the ark of his covenant, and the principles of a purer church, and a better state, than had been vouchsafed to the world before.

2. The Pilgrims established here *Pure and Free Churches*.

The Reformed Churches of Europe had so recently come out of the darkness of the Middle Ages and the corruptions of the Papal Church, that perhaps it is not strange that they brought with them so many of the errors and superstitions of

3

those times. Even the English Church was only imperfectly reformed. It was the attempt to bring back the medieval faith, and especially those forms of worship and that extent of priestly and church power, which caused the sufferings of the non-conformists, and the flight of so many from England.

Our fathers held that the Bible was a sufficient rule of faith and practice, and that men had a right to read and to interpret it, responsible only to God. Whatever that book taught, they regarded themselves under obligation to receive; and whatever they understood it to forbid, they considered it wrong, for either the Church or the State, to require. Upon this ground of religious freedom as one of the rights of men, they refused conscientiously to conform to some of the practices of the Church, and some the requirements of the State, and rather than do it preferred to submit to all the pains and penalties of non-conformity.

They also went back in the organization of their own churches to the model of the New Testament churches, and sought to bring them as near as possible to the form of church government found there. Instead of forming their several Christian congregations into one great church establishment, like the church of England, or the church of Rome, they organized them as separate churches, such as "the church at Jerusalem," and "the church at Antioch," "the church of God which is at Corinth," and "the church which is at Cencrea," the port of Corinth; "the church of the Laodiceans," and "the church which is in Nympha's house." Instead of having them governed by the State, or by any class of men, whether ecclesiastics or laymen, they were allowed to govern themselves; as "the multitude of the disciples" at Jerusalem were called together and chose deacons, when such a class of men were needed, instead of their being appointed by the apostles, and as Paul instructs the church at Corinth, when they "are gathered together," to excommunicate one who was walking unworthily, instead of doing it himself. They organized them upon the basis of independency and self-government; each church independent, in all spiritual affairs, of the State, and of all hierarchies, and capable within itself, and by the voice of its own members, of electing its own officers, and administering its own discipline, and managing all its affairs.

Their theory of church government was the democratic one. They recognized in every fellow Christian, without regard to his condition, or color, or attainments, one originally of the same parentage, redeemed by the same great sacrifice, and renewed by the same divine grace, and therefore having his own inherent dignity and rights, and entitled to consideration and regard. While they had so little respect for the divine right of kings, and no more for ministers and bishops on account of their apostolic succession, they cherished a profound regard for every fellow-creature as made in God's image, and especially for every truly saintly soul, as a child of God, and a disciple of his Son, and willingly gave him a place in all their deliberations and decisions. This is what led so naturally and necessarily to a democratic form of civil government. It was this high regard for man as man, and for his natural rights; they held his capacities in such high honor, and had such faith in his integrity, especially when piety was once implanted in his heart, that they did not hesitate to intrust with him responsibility and power. While others regarded the mass of the people as incapable of adopting their own religious faith, and unfit to have any voice in the government of the Church and the State, they deemed them qualified to do both. Though their views of native depravity, and man's moral character, were rigidly Calvinistic, such were their notions about human dignity, and capabilities and rights. And when they came to organize their churches, and found their commonwealth, they based them upon thoroughly democratic principles, and incorporated these principles into the whole frame-work of both Church and State. The idea used to be that the mass of the people were not capable of forming their own religious opinions, but the church must dictate to them their faith, and the civil power must lend its aid to make them receive it. And they could never be trusted to provide for their own spiritual wants, and organize their own churches, and support them, and regulate their own worship and discipline, and that without any resort to the aid of the civil power.

Complete separation of the Church from the State, the Puritans, when they came over, had not quite reached. It was embraced in their principles of church government, and naturally, and in time, would grow out of them. But this, and perfect religious toleration, were only the fruit of that seed, which they had sown so long, and cultivated so assiduously, and which it required time enough to ripen. True the churches at first were supported by the State, and what might be deemed moral delinquencies, or ecclesiastical offences, were sometimes punished by civil statutes. In some of the colonies, as in this, church membership was necessary to make one a voter. But in others, as in the Plymouth, and Connecticut colonies, this was never required. All such things, however, were violations of their own principles of religious freedom, and they could never justify them, and in time they would be done away. Their churches were in theory free churches, and would eventually become such in fact, while they were independent, and self-governed, and admitting all their brethren to share in that government.

And as showing what such churches can be, and do, our fathers may be said to have made a great and successful experiment. The religious interests of this nation, cannot be said to have been neglected, even if neither the State, nor any great ecclesiastical establishment looks after them. It is found that churches can be built by voluntary means, almost wherever they are needed, and that they can be supported, without any aid from the State, or enforced taxation. It is one of the marvels of this land to a foreigner, as it was lately to that Congregational delegation from England to our National Council, that they could look off, as one of them said, from Northampton upon a rural landscape that brought within view the spires of twenty-two churches, and as the other said, he could count in another landscape seventeen churches, glistening in the sunlight, all built and supported by private contributions, and proofs of the value we set upon the gospel, and its institutions and influences. The truth is, when a people can be once made to appreciate such institutions, they will provide themselves with them, and do it with a cheerfulness and liberality which no ecclesiastical organization, or national government, could be expected to exercise, and the voluntary principle may be relied upon for such work, as superior to any other. And then these churches have not fallen into all manner of errors and extravagances, as would have been predicted. With their government a perfect democracy, and with their brief creeds, and simple organization, they remain—with a partial exception in this Commonwealth—substantially in faith and order what the Pilgrim Fathers organized them. And as for intelligent theology, and exemplary piety, and practical benevolence, the results will compare favorably, to say the least, with those of any ecclesiastical establishment, or state religion.

The influence of such principles, and such churches, has virtually made all churches in this land free and well nigh self-governed. Our fathers protest against ecclesiastical and civil usurpation:—their principles of religious liberty and self-government; the inherent justice of such government and liberty; and especially the happy results of such an organization; have commended them to the regard, and more

3*

or less to the adoption, of all our churches and denominations. What church, or denomination, does not now rejoice in the perfect religious toleration which exists here? Which of them would, if it could, connect the church with the State again? How much there is of self-government, in all of them, and in each individual church? Even where so much power is nominally in the Pope, or the Bishop, or the Session, how seldom it is exercised without any regard to the convictions and wishes of the people? What Session is likely to administer church discipline without consulting in some measure the judgment of the whole brotherhood? When a Bishop appoints a rector to a church, or assigns a preacher to a station, how much deference is sure to be paid after all to the choice of those to whom they are sent? Even the head of the Papal Church, and all its ecclesiastics, have much more respect for the popular voice, and the convictions of the people, in this land than in Europe. The churches here are all of them comparatively free, and more or less self-governed. And this has come about, in no small measure, from the ecclesiastical principles and practice of the Puritans. So that all who set any value upon religious liberty owe them a debt of gratitude, in common with the rest of us, whatever may be their faith or forms of worship.

What a blessed result this is! To enjoy religious freedom, and be no longer persecuted for our faith. To fear neither the stake, nor banishment, nor fine, nor imprisonment! To have the Church separated from the State, and be no longer disqualified for any civil office by our religious convictions, nor taxed to support doctrines that we believe false, and forms of church government that we deem corrupting and oppressive! To know that every little company of believers may be safely trusted to take care of their own creed, and discipline their own number, and with the other churches of their own denomination, and with other Christian denominations, may be left to support religious institutions, and to plant them eventually wherever they are needed, over the whole length and breadth of this land! This is a result that deserves to be appreciated, and the men that had so much to do with securing it, ought to be held in high honor.

3. The Pilgrims also made this nation a *Republic.*

There is only one step from self-government in the Church, to self-government in the State. But there had always been the same false reasoning about both, and the incapacity of the people to govern themselves in either. "The people elect their own rulers, and make their own laws! They do not know enough. If they did, they have not principle enough. They are creatures of prejudice and passion. They will be always given to change. They will elect ignorant men, or unprincipled men, to office. They will demand unwise legislation, and refuse to obey the laws which their own legislators have enacted. Such a government will be as unstable as the sea, and liable to be swept away by every change of popular sentiment." So the world thought, and so it reasoned. Even the people themselves had come to believe that they could not govern themselves, but must have kings to rule over them, and nobles to represent them, and a few statesmen to carry on the government for them; just as in religious matters, the priesthood, and the bishops, and the church, and the Pope, must tell them what to believe, and teach them how to worship, and prescribe what they must do in order to be saved. But our fathers had arrived at the conviction, that in spiritual things this was neither necessary, nor safe, nor right. So they had based their churches upon different principles. And having found that it could be done, and that it worked well, they proposed to model their Commonwealth after their church. If the people might be trusted to adopt their own creed, why might they not be allowed to choose their own rulers? If they could organize and administer church government, why should they not make and administer their civil laws? True, it would require intelligence, and moral principle, to do this. But what of that? If they must be educated, let this be done. And if they must be virtuous, as well as intelligent, let moral and religious influences be multiplied and stimulated till they are qualified in this respect for their duty. This was the way they reasoned, and they were bold enough in founding a new State, to carry out these principles into practice.

When they left Holland, as appears from the letter of advice, which their pastor, John Robinson, gave them at parting, they proposed "to become a body politic, using amongst themselves civil government, and to choose their own rulers from among themselves."—(Young's Chron., p. 95 and 121.) And when they arrived on the coast, the day before they came to anchor, they drew up and signed this formal compact:

" In the name of God, Amen. We, whose names are underwritten, the loyal subjects of our dread sovereign lord, King James, by the grace of God, of Great Britain, France and Ireland King, defender of the faith, &c., having undertaken, for the glory of God, and advancement of the Christian faith, and honor of our king and country, a voyage to plant the first colony in the northern part of Virginia, do, by these presents, solemnly and mutually, in the presence of God and of one another, covenant and combine ourselves together into a civil body politic, for our better ordering and preservation, and furtherance of the ends aforesaid; and by virtue hereof to enact, constitute and frame such just and equal laws, ordinances, acts, constitutions, and offices, from time to time, as shall be thought most meet and convenient for the general good of the colony; unto which we promise all due submission and obedience. In witness whereof, we have hereunder subscribed our names, at Cape Cod, the 11th of November, in the year of the reign of our sovereign lord, King James, of England, France and Ireland, the eighteenth, and of Scotland the fifty-fourth, Anno Domini 1620." And here follow their signatures, in behalf of themselves and their families, making and representing 101 persons in all. Thus our government was born in the cabin of the Mayflower, and out of the throes and anguish of those patient and hopeful souls, and when they first stepped ashore, they brought the child in their arms, the most cherished one of all their company.

"Here," as has been remarked, "for the first time in the world's history, the philosophical fiction of a social compact was realized in practice." They undertook to carry out their principles, and made their government a republic. It was to be a government of the people. The people were to elect their own rulers, and make their own laws. From this would naturally follow all the peculiarities of a popular government. While they recognized the king, under whose charter they were planting their colony, their form of government would require no hereditary ruler, nor long admit of any privileged classes. It recognized man's capacity to govern himself, and claimed for him certain rights, which neither the King nor Parliament might take from him without his consent, or when forfeited by some crime. All this was naturally wrapped up in the very germ of a popular government. The other New England governments were like this essentially. And from these has been derived confessedly the peculiar form of our National and State governments. As *De Tocqueville*, one of the ablest and most candid of those who have written upon our institutions, has said : "Two or three main ideas, which constitute the basis of the social theory of the United States, were first combined in the northern British colonies, more generally denominated the states of New England. The principles of New England spread at first to the neighboring

States; then they passed successively to the more distant ones; and at length they imbued the whole confederation. They now extend their influence beyond its limits, over the whole American world. The civilization of New England has been like a beacon lit upon a hill, which, after it has diffused its warmth around, tinges the distant horizon with its glow."

Now to have demonstrated the success of such an experiment, and upon such a scale ; to have proved this whole people capable of self-government, and not merely a colony of Puritans, but men of so many different nationalities and religions ; to have shown such principles, securing to men so many of their rights, and after a conflict with opposing principles of two centuries and a half, coming off at last victorious, and emancipating four millions of slaves ; to have exhibited this form of government, affording as much of protection and security as most governments, and infinitely more of contentment, and prosperity, and development such as freedom gives, than any of them ; to have spread such a government across the continent, and united in itself so many different and distant states ; to have this government proved wise and prudent, where such qualities are called for, and when energy and valor are required, to have such virtues exhibited ; and to have been shown strong in a great national emergency, just where we were supposed to be the weakest, and "not only able to conquer our enemies in the field, but also to govern ourselves in the hour of victory ;" this is no ordinary or unimportant achievement. It is a grand experiment made for all time, and for the race. Already despots tremble, and the oppressed look up with hope. The nations are claiming, and their rulers are conceding to them, more of their rights. Reforms, and constitutional securities, are being yielded to the people, and in the light of our success, it seems to look as if civil and religious freedom were likely to spread somewhat rapidly among the nations, and the world's political millennium at length to dawn.

4. The Pilgrims also established here a system of *popular and universal education.*

The notion that "Ignorance is the mother of devotion" is a Papal, and not a Puritan idea. Their very starting-point in religion, that men are responsible for their own religious faith, and must not receive error from any one, not less than their conviction, that men must be intelligent, to be qualified for self-government, either in Church or State, led alike to the same conclusion. They must be educated. They must all be educated. And this must be done at the public expense, if necessary. For an ignorant people are no more fit to be entrusted with republican institutions, than a corrupt and un-principled population are. One of the reasons which they gave for leaving Holland was that they could not properly educate their children there.

Accordingly we find the first settlers, wherever they plant a settlement, erecting a church, and a school-house by the side of it. This illustrates the connection and friendship be-tween the two in their minds. Religion favors education, and education promotes religion. They early established a college at Cambridge, and out of their poverty provided for its support, and it was especially to educate men for the minis-try, for, as one of them said, " we cannot bear, when our minis-ters are in their graves, that all learning shall be buried in the same grave with them." Within twenty-five years after the first settlement of New England, there were not less than eighty ministers—one for every two hundred, or two hundred and fifty inhabitants—dwelling in the few villages of Massa-chusetts and Connecticut. Half of them are known to have been graduates of Oxford, or Cambridge in England, the greater part being of the latter University. And some of them had been eminent for their talents and attainments at home, before they came over, and had shared in the counsels and the conflicts of the Puritan leaders, during some of the most critical periods of English history.—(Palfrey's History, Vol. 2.)

In strange contrast with this, was the ignorance of the clergy of the Church of England, not fifty years before. When the best ministers were driven out of the Church for non-conformity, "the body of the conforming clergy,"—we are told, " were so ignorant and illiterate, that many who had the cure of souls, were incapable of preaching, or even of reading to the edification of the hearers."—(Neale, Vol. 1, p. 230.)   "In the County of Cornwall there were one hundred and forty clergymen, not one of which was capable of preaching a sermon."—(p. 245.) It was for such men that a liturgy was very properly prepared, and they were required to confine themselves to the use of it. Forms of prayers were prescribed for their use. And homilies were also provided to be read instead of sermons. So long as they could not pray with propriety, or preach to edification, this was necessary, and was a good arrangement for such ministers.

But our fathers provided for themselves from the first an educated ministry. And they determined that the whole body of the people should possess all the element of knowledge, or at least be able to read for themselves the Word of God. This they deemed the natural birthright of every child. And if he could come into possession of it in no other way, it should be furnished at the expense of the State.

The common school system of education, is derived from Geneva, where Calvin was the author of it. Thence it was introduced by John Knox into Scotland, as it was into Germany by Luther, and from Scotland our ancestors derived it, and transplanted it to this soil.—(Bancroft.) Here it has had a vigorous growth, and is assuming vast proportions, and the leaves of it, next to those of the Tree of Life, are for the healing of the nation.

No one can estimate the results in time, of this single one of our Puritan institutions. It is already giving New England, and the Northern States, a decided superiority over the South, and when it shall have equally blessed the South with the North, and helped to elevate every class of each section, even the ignorant freedman, and the poor whites, as well as the children of the newly arrived emigrant, and most favored son of the soil, then will it be shown what freedom and education can do for a people, and how with virtue and piety, they can rise in the scale of nations, leaving all ignorant, and oppressed, and godless nations infinitely below them.

5. And finally, the Pilgrims have founded a *great empire.*

The natural inheritance which our fathers received was a rare one. With a territory of such extent, stretching across the entire continent, and capable of furnishing a home for so many millions; with such varieties of soil and climate, and productions, and with native resources and capabilities that seem infinite and inexhaustible; with such an extent of sea-coast and lakes, and rivers, and every facility for trade and commerce; with such mineral wealth, and stores of coal and iron, and abundance of water-power, and the easy production of cotton, that great staple of manufactures and commerce; to have received such a country for their home, and when it was all unoccupied, and required no conquests to put them into possession of it, as our fathers did, was the grandest inheritance that ever fell to the founders of any nation. The Land of Canaan, good as it was, and great as it became under Jewish institutions and the divine blessing, was small in extent, and limited in its resources, compared with this. Greece was small indeed for so many states, and to be the seat of so much literature and art. Italy, though larger, and far richer

4

in soil, and climate, and sea-coast, and productions, compelled the Roman Empire to be essentially one of colonies. The British Isles are insignificantly small and limited in their resources for such a kingdom. Even the Russian Empire, grand as it is territorially, is in many parts barren and uninhabitable, or lies too near the cold of Siberia. Ours is, in a higher sense than any of them, " a good land," and the angel of God's presence that went before our fathers, and guided them hither, might have been heard cheering them along their tedious journeyings, and saying, " For the Lord thy God bringeth thee into a good land, a land of brooks of water, of fountains and depths that spring out of valleys and hills ; a land of wheat, and barley, and vines, and pomegranates, a land of oil-olive and honey ; a land wherein thou shalt eat bread without scarceness ; thou shalt not lack anything in it ; a land whose stones are iron, and out of whose hills thou mayest dig brass."

Here a nation of thirty-six states, and numerous territories, and a population of thirty million, has been called into existence. And it is not a nation of Asiatics, with the institutions of Confusius, or the religion of Brahma, but of European, and Protestant, and Puritan origin, with Christianity for its religion, and all the elements and influences of a Christian civilization. In most of the elements of national greatness, such as agriculture, manufactures, commerce, literature, arts and arms, we may be said to compare favorably with other nations, and already rank among the first class powers. While in other respects, such as the freedom given and safely given to the people ; the regard paid to human rights, irrespective of birth, or condition, or complexion ; the industry, thrift and contentment of our population ; and the disposition of the people to provide for their own religious wants, and their ability to do it for themselves better than the State, or any Church or State establishment could do it for them ; in these respects, it is no boasting to say that we have surpassed them all. This is confessedly the land of invitation to the poor of all nations, the asylum of the oppressed, the model in many respects of reformers and wise statesmen, the dream of philosophers, and the hope of patriots and Christians the world over. And this has all been the outgrowth of Puritanism and its principles, within two centuries and a half.

And when such results are more fully realized, and our population shall have stretched across the entire continent, scattering over it comfortable homes, and elegant residences, and pleasant villages, and thrifty towns, and magnificent cities; when this landscape is dotted over with churches, and school-houses, and institutions of charity, and all the outgrowth of a higher civilization, and a purer Christianity; when the long sought route from Europe to the Indies, shall be found to lie across this continent, and along it shall pour the travel of Europe, and the traffic of Asia, and in exchange for both shall be carried back Puritan ideas, and influences and institutions, by far the best part of the transaction; then shall it be seen what an Empire the pilgrims were founding.

What if it does become large; too large, as many think, to be ever embraced under one government. With our present system of intercommunication perfected, it will never be practically so large as our original Union of thirteen States. When the Pacific Railroad is finished, San Francisco will in reality be nearer to Washington, than Portland was to the seat of the first Congress. Our system is meant to expand, and is capable of it to almost any extent. Each State is within its own sphere, independent and self-governed, and so is every town. And as our safety, and prosperity and power, must so much of it depend upon our union, so long as the nation can be made to realize it; and we know not why the people cannot be made to understand this, as well as anything else of public interest; we see no reason why this should not continue to be one nation, and constitute a great and growing Empire.

It is grand already, but grander still in its future. When England, two centuries ago, was carrying forward the Reformation in Church and State, and laying the foundations of her present greatness and glory, Milton, with the insight of genius, and almost the foresight of a prophet, exclaimed: "Methinks I see in my mind a noble and puissant nation rousing herself like a strong man after sleep, and shaking her invincible locks; methinks I see her as an eagle nursing her mighty youth, and kindling her undazzled eyes at the full mid-day beam; purging and unsealing her long abused sight at the fountain itself of heavenly radiance; while the whole noise of timorous and flocking birds, with those also that love the twilight, flutter about, amazed at what she means, and in their envious gabble prognosticate a failure." But what gave to England her vigor and her promise then, is ours now, and more. Her protestant faith, her constitutional government, and so many just and Christian ideas incorporated into her laws, as well as the blood and spirit of Englishmen, belong to us for the most part, as well as to them; while we have got rid of many of her errors and wrongs, and are no longer burdened with kings and aristocracies, nor cursed with religious intolerance, and State Churches, and hierarchies. And with better institutions, founded upon juster principles, and breathing more of the spirit of Christianity, and with a nobler field for their development, than a nation ever had before; is it self-conceit, or blind enthusiasm, that look so hopefully upon our future? Is it anything so very strange, that the eaglet, so pecked at, and hawked at, and driven from the nest, after being compelled to fly across the ocean, and find a home for itself here, and accustomed to dwell amid such solitudes, and range over a continent for its prey, should now beat the air with a mightier wing, and mount still nearer to the sun, than any that were left behind? With truer ideas, and juster principles, and a better opportunity to incorporate them into the whole frame-work of society, and with such conviction of their truth and justice, and with such sacrifices to work them out successfully, and with God's blessing which has crowned the enterprise from the beginning, are these results anything surprising, or are our hopes for the future visionary? The Empire which our fathers founded, has become great already, but it looks grander in the future.

Such are some of the results of that Pilgrim Emigration. These men have founded and built up a great Christian Commonwealth, where the people enjoy more of the blessings of good government, and where they suffer fewer wrongs, and where more of the spirit of Christianity is incorporated into its institutions and legislation, than was ever known before. In these respects, it must be admitted to be an improvement upon anything in the past, and that the results show it to be a great advance in human society. It has been shown that a people can govern themselves, and do it better than kings and nobles would do it for them. It has been proved that they may safely enjoy an amount of civil and religious freedom—freedom of conscience, freedom of speech, freedom of the press, freedom of the pulpit—which used to be deemed utterly inconsistent with the welfare of society, and the safety of the church. It has been seen that the mass of the people can find out truth, as well as some particular class or body of men, and are quite as likely to be honest in their inquiries. It has become apparent also that the people can appreciate their own religious wants, and provide for them, better than the State, or any State Church, can do it. It is evident that they can value industry, and enterprise, and temperance, and domestic virtues, and education, and piety, and do as much to foster each, as any other form of government whatever. It is plain that individual enterprise and voluntary organizations,

4*

and the vigorous competition which freedom creates, are adequate to undertakings, and capable of achievements, such as no absolute despotism, with the amplest resources, would ever dream of accomplishing. And it is also clear that our form of government adapts itself readily to reforms, and can easily correct its own mistakes and abuses, and even slough out such a cancer as slavery, better than any other. And when we have nobly passed through such a revolution and civil war as has just been brought to a close, and have proved ourselves the strongest in such an emergency where we were supposed to be the weakest, and shown ourselves as temperate in victory as we had been patient under defeat, and as magnanimous toward the conquered as we had proved formidable to them as foes; it has been shown, beyond all further controversy, that those old Puritan ideas were more just, and such institutions more valuable to mankind, than any that had preceded them, or have since been substituted for them. And were this Republic to be broken up to-day, it would still be true that such a form of government, and such freedom in civil matters and in religion, were the best for society that had yet been discovered, and that nation would show itself the wisest which should copy this model the closest, and carry out such ideas in its institutions and legislation. Our failure would only prove that we were incapable of adhering to the principles which our fathers bequeathed us. And we should hope, for the sake of truth, and righteousness, and the interests of mankind, and the Divine glory, that some nation would be found to work out the problem of human government upon these principles still more successfully.

In view of such results and achievements we should certainly *honor the memory of our Pilgrim Fathers.*

The founders of great empires are held in high regard. Peter the Great, and Alfred the Wise, will never be forgotten in Russia and England, so long as those kingdoms flourish.

Virgil composed his Æneid, in honor of the men who first settled Italy, and became the founders of the Roman Empire. And indebted as we are to these men for better institutions, and a purer faith, and a nobler kingdom, and one as we trust with a higher destiny, than any of them, we may well admire their work and cherish their memory.

They were men of course, and with more or less of the imperfections and faults, and mistakes of men. But as compared with others of their own age—the only fair way to judge of them—they stand out far in advance of their generation, for their discernment of just and important principles, and the value which they attached to them, and the consistency with which they clung to them, and the sufferings they endured in behalf of them, and the practical application which they successfully made of them ; and above all, for the spirit of faith and benevolence in which they did this, when there was so much in their circumstances to discourage and embitter them. In these respects they were as superior to those about them as Saul was above all the rest of Israel : " From his shoulders and upward, he was higher than any of the people."

Look at the spirit which they manifested in respect to truth and duty ; could anything be nobler? It was as far removed from a contempt for old truths, as from prejudice against any new one ; as profound a reverence for divine teaching, as it was a fearless disregard of human errors ; neither obstinately conservative, nor recklessly radical, deeming, as they say, " nothing old that will not stand by the word of God, and nothing new that will." What could be more wise, or judicious, or candid, or catholic, than the farewell advice of their pastor, John Robinson, when they were about to begin the " great work of plantation in New England." " We are now ere long to part asunder," as one of them reports it, " and the Lord knoweth whether ever he should live to see our faces again. But whether the Lord hath appointed it or not, he charged us before God and his blessed angels, to follow him no further than he followed Christ; and if God should reveal anything to us by any other instrument of his, to be as ready to receive it as ever we were to receive any truths by his ministry; for he was very confident the Lord had more truth and light yet to break forth out of his holy word. He took occasion also miserably to bewail the state and condition of the Reformed Churches, who were come to a period in religion, and would go no further than the instruments of their reformation. As, for example, the Lutherans, they could not be drawn to go beyond what Luther said; for whatever part of God's will he had further imparted and revealed to Calvin, they will rather die than embrace it. And so also, saith he, you see the Calvinists, they stick where he left them — a misery much to be lamented; for though they were precious shining lights in their times, yet God had not revealed his whole will to them; and were they now living, saith he, they would be as ready and willing to embrace further light, as that they had received. Here also he puts us in mind of our church covenant, at least that part of it whereby we promise and covenant with God and one with another, to receive whatsoever light or truth shall be made known to us from his written word; but withal exhorted us to take heed what we received for truth, and well to examine and compare it and weigh it with other Scriptures of truth before we receive it. For, saith he, it is not possible the Christian world should come so lately out of such thick anti-Christian darkness, and that full perfection of knowledge should break forth at once."—(Young's Chron., p. 397.)

"How astonishing," as has been said, "are such words, in that age of low and universal bigotry, which then prevailed in the English nation, wherein this truly great and learned man seems to be the only divine who was capable of rising into a noble freedom of thinking and practicing in religious matters, and even of urging such an equal liberty on his own people. He labors to take them off from their attachment to him, that they might be more entirely free to search and follow the Scriptures."

Talk about the bigotry and superstition of those men! The truth is, they had the least of such base qualities of any people of that age, and less than most have now. They believed in witches, but they were among the first to outgrow such inherited notions. Just before that time belief in witchcraft was universal, and the laws punished it as a crime, and such a judge as Sir Mathew Hale did not hesitate to condemn persons to death for it. It is estimated that not less than 30,000 persons were capitally executed in Great Britain within two centuries, and such things took place there as late as 1722, a quarter of a century after any such thing was known in New England. And yet forsooth, our fathers were such miserable fanatics, when just a score, all told, perished in that Salem excitement! Besides it must be admitted, that while witches were put to death in this Colony, none are known to have been executed for such offences, in either of the other colonies. While there were several colonies, there was only one of them which was carried away by this superstitious frenzy, and then only for a short time, after which it was regretted and bewailed in the most contrite manner. There were many ministers, but only one Cotton Mather, who while such a scholar, and so full of lore, was quite deficient in sound judgment.

And to make one man and one community, and during a season of popular excitement, the representative of all the rest, and of the universal and permanent public sentiment of those times, would be almost as unjust, as to represent the border ruffianism which swept over Kansas a few years ago, as the spirit of this nation, and one of the fixed characteristics of our population. Are they to be singled out as superstitious, who only shared in a delusion of the times, and were so soon to rise above it and leave all such laws as dead letters upon their statute books? And were they of all men such bigots?—so wedded to their creed, and devoted to their sect, that not even God's commands could ever alter their opinions, or change their religous connections? Were those men bigots, who could talk like that Puritan minister to his flock, or who would listen to such preaching, and approve of it too, as they did? Bigots are not wont to be so anxious to know the truth, and so willing to receive it from any quarter, and so ready to join themselves to any communion, only let it be a communion of saints, and the authority of God which justifies it. If such men were bigots, where shall we look for conscientious and candid seekers after truth, in that or any other age?

But were they not an ascetic and vulgar people, intolerant and persecuting, and enacting laws which were a disgrace to any civilized and Christian community? They did pass laws that seem strange to us now, and some of them, especially some borrowed from the Jewish system, and such as punished ecclesiastical offences with civil penalties, and such as undertook to regulate personal morals, and what would be called sumptuary laws, we have found out to be unwise, if not a violation of their own principles. The principles of religious freedom were only imperfectly understood then, especially the limits of that freedom, and mistakes were made in the application of them, and more than all, our fathers, like the rest of us, did not always act up to their own principles. Still their legislation will compare favorably with that of any nation in those days, and was meant to be pre-eminently paternal and Christian. They did persecute Roger Williams, and punish the Quakers. But it is due to truth to say, that while Massachusetts banished Williams, he found a shelter and kindess in the Plymouth Colony, though they always regarded him as a very uncomfortable man to get along with. And it was as cruel, as it was unwise, to treat the Quakers as they did, though they were such miserable fanatics and disturbers of the peace. The amount of it is, that they violated their own better principles, and under provocation were guilty of conduct which they ought to have been ashamed of, and probably were, just as we are ashamed of having suppressed in our day freedom of speech, and mobbed men for advocating an unpopular cause. And as for their asceticisms and vulgarity ; those were stern and sober times, and they had little opportunity, if they had possessed the disposition, to cultivate the graces and accomplishments of what was then deemed courtly society. If they were not such gallants as the men of Charles the Second's time, they had better morals. If they sang psalms and hymns, and sang through their noses— which certainly was not in good taste—it was probably quite as much for their edification, and as acceptable to God, as if it had been some vulgar song of that day, and better executed. If they bore uncouth Scripture names, and wore their hair cut short, and dressed with less taste than some gay cavalier, they were quite as likely to find their names written in the Lamb's Book of Life, and to be clothed in "the fine linen which is the righteousness of saints."

To judge of things according to their comparative worth, and by the standard of the Gospel, what are such trifles by the side of the noble characteristics and sublime virtues of the Puritans ? Are they to be estimated, especially in this Christian age, according to their manners, and dress, instead of their moral worth and heroic achievements ? Very likely your mother was not so handsome and fashionable a woman as some that shone at Charles' Court ; but she had more virtue than the whole of them, a..? trained you to a better faith, and a nobler life. Is it not almost time to be done with such paltry criticisms, and whoever else makes them, let it not be one of their own children.* Let others trace their blood, if they will, back to some licentious cavalier, or persecuting lord, but I prefer a Christian origin, and to claim a descent from the Puritans; men who feared God, and taught me to fear him, and loved their fellow-men, and taught me to love them, and set me such an example of devoted piety, and of life-long sacrifice for the good of others.

> " 'Tis not that I derive my birth
> From loins enthroned, and rulers of the earth ;
> But higher yet my proud pretensions rise—
> The child of parents passed into the skies."

We also do well to *value the principles and maintain the institutions of the Pilgrims.*

If these principles are entitled to respect, it is because they are true and just ; and if these institutions have any peculiar worth, it is because they are better than others, and can do more for society and the church. And the world has need enough of their influence. Is the truth never to be free? Are men never to have their rights? Are they never to be trusted to govern themselves, not even God's saints? Must they be forever treated as children, and never entrusted with responsibilities, and never allowed any opportunity for devel-

---

* Is it not time to understand that what was meant as fair ridicule of the foibles of the Puritans, and what was designedly a malicious slander upon the Pilgrims, is not historic truth ? Thus, when Hume gives in a note a list of the names of a Round-head jury, said to have been empaneled in those days, made up of such as Praisegod Barebones, and the like, it is easy to see that it was got up by some of the wits of that age, and must have answered a good purpose in checking a practice that was becoming ridiculous. And so when we hear, as we still do, of "The Blue Laws of Connecticut," it ought to be known that no such code ever existed as has been published under that name, and some of whose most absurd enactments are in the memory and on the tongue of everybody, but that it was the work of one Peters, a tory, who left this country in disgust, and first published the slander in England, to revenge himself upon a community that despised him. He says himself that these laws were never suffered to be printed.

opment, but doomed to perpetual babyhood, for fear that somebody will believe something wrong, or do something bad? Must a few govern all the rest, when they have never done it any too well, or a few dictate their faith to all others, who have shown themselves none too free from prejudice and error?

The nations have been making some progress in these respects, but, alas, how slowly! The bulk of mankind to-day have no faith whatever in any kind of freedom. Of all Christendom, not a tithe of the people are yet satisfied that Christianity may be left to take care of itself, and fight its own battles. Of Protestant nations, there are but few that are yet rid of Church and State establishments, and Ecclesiastical Hierarchies, and Spiritual Despotisms. Even in our own country, the principles of civil and religious liberty, and especially of self-government in the Church, are only imperfectly understood and carried out; while there has hitherto been one entire section of the land where Puritan ideas, and Puritan churches were with difficulty planted. And when the whole nation so needs them, and would be so improved by them; and when the world needs their influence, and they would so bless her struggling millions; and when here at home such ideas need to be more fully developed, and more thoroughly wrought out, and more happily exemplified; it is for us to give such an exemplification of them, and apply them better, and do more to disseminate them over the land and over the world.

When, therefore, it is proposed, on this Anniversary of the Landing of the Pilgrims, to aid in building churches after the Puritan model, and helping to scatter them over the length and breadth of the land, we do well to join in such an appropriate and useful work. Let them be multiplied, until whatever virtue there is in such ideas and such institutions shall be shared in by all our population. Let them rise, till the Puritan faith, and self-government, and freedom, and re-

gard for learning, and estimate of piety, shall be embodied
and exhibited in their easy working and blessed influence, to
every observer. Let such influences spread over all the land,
like the breath of spring, till "the wilderness and the solitary
place shall be glad for them, and the desert shall rejoice and
blossom as the rose, and the glory of Lebanon shall be given
unto it, the excellency of Carmel and Sharon." Let them
spread, until peace and plenty, industry and contentment, intelligence and piety, flourish everywhere, as they do under
the blessing of Heaven, and as flowers spring up, and fruits
ripen, and men rejoice, wherever the sunshine reaches.

When the Israelites passed over Jordan, and came into
possession of the Promised Land, they gathered stones out of
the bed of the stream, and piled them into a heap upon the
shore, as a memorial of that great event in their history,
and out of gratitude for God's interposition and mercies.
"And it came to pass when all the people were clean gone
over Jordan, that the Lord spake unto Joshua, saying : ' Take
you twelve men out of the people, out of every tribe a man,
and command ye them, saying : "Take ye hence out of the
midst of Jordan, out of the place where the priest's feet stood
firm, twelve stones, and ye shall carry them over with you,
and leave them in the lodging-place where ye shall lodge this
night." ' Then Joshua called the twelve men whom he had
prepared of the children of Israel, out of every tribe a
man, and Joshua said unto them : ' Pass over before the Ark
of the Lord your God into the midst of Jordan, and take ye
up every man of you a stone upon his shoulder, according
unto the number of the tribes of Israel, that this may be a
sign unto you, that when your children ask their fathers
in time to come, saying : ' What mean ye by these stones ?'
Then ye shall answer them: ' That the waters of Jordan
were cut off and these stones shall be a memorial unto the
children of Israel forever.' " In a like spirit, we who are
descendants of the Pilgrims, and revere their memory, and

value their institutions, out of gratitude for our inheritance, propose, in connection with all the churches of our denomination in the land, to make a free-will offering to build up their religious faith and church polity, and especially to aid in building houses of worship for churches of like faith and polity, in the destitute parts of the country.

We propose no useless monument to their memory, but to preserve their institutions and extend their influence. This land is their monument. When the traveler visits St. Paul's Cathedral, and looks around for a monument to its architect, as he gazes up into its magnificent dome, he reads this inscription—" Si Monumentum requiris, circumspice ;" [If you seek his monument, look around you.] So their best memorial, is the land they have settled and blessed. Look around you, and see what a good land they selected for their settlement, and when it shall have been more fully possessed and developed, what a magnificent inheritance it will have become for a people. Look around you, and see what a large, and thrifty, and intelligent, and virtuous, and happy population, are already settled here, and how all the evidences of a higher Christian civilization abound. Look around, and see this population self-governed, the people electing their own rulers, and making their own laws, and as well governed, and more contented, than any other nation on the globe. Look around, and see the amount of liberty that is granted to every individual ; liberty of conscience, and speech, and press, and pulpit ; and how safely it is granted. Look around, and see what regard is paid to human rights, and how much more respect is paid to man, and to his personal character and worth, than to such accidents as birth, and position, and complexion. Look around, and see what provision is made for public education, and how the poor, as well as the rich are provided with this choice gift, and how in theory, and eventually almost in fact, it is to become the inheritance of every citizen. Look around, and see perfect religious toleration, and so many pure and earnest churches, doing so much for themselves, and the land, and the world, and God, and this with no help from the State, and with so little interference from the State, or from any ecclesiastical establishment, or from any class of men, or from any quarter whatever. Look around, and see this vast and growing empire, powerful already in all the elements of national strength and mightier still in its glowing future. And now tell us, when did ever men rear for themselves, or have reared for them, such a monument! And seeing what has come, under God, of that pilgrim emigration, that disembarked upon Plymouth Rock on that winter's day, and what we owe to such a parentage, and for such an inheritance, we bow reverently, and lift up our hearts to Heaven and give thanks.

" Thou has brought a vine out of Egypt, thou hast cast out the heathen and planted it. Thou preparedst room before it, and did cause it to take deep root, and it filled the land. The hills were covered with the shadow of it, and the boughs thereof were like goodly cedars."

" Then said they among the heathen, ' The Lord hath done great things for them.' The Lord hath done great things for us whereof we are glad."

" Blessed be the Lord, that hath given rest unto his people Israel, according to all that he promised. The Lord our God be with us, as he was with our fathers. Let him not leave us, nor forsake us ; that he may incline our hearts unto him, to walk in all his ways, and to keep his commandments and his statutes, and his judgments, which he commanded our fathers ; that all the people of the earth may know that the Lord is God, and that there is none else."

" Thy fathers went down into Egypt with threescore and ten persons, and now the Lord thy God hath made thee as the stars of heaven for multitude. Therefore thou shalt love the Lord thy God, and keep his charge, and his statutes, and his judgments, and his commandments, always."